A Mixed bag
Short Stories

By Fraser Aseltine

Disclaimer. This is a work of fiction. Names, characters, business, events and incidents are the products of the author's imagination. Any resemblance to actual persons, living or dead, or actual events is purely coincidental.

Contents

Badge of Merit

"It's a great honour, sir. Your father would have been proud of you - after all, there aren't many who are awarded the Military Medal," the young Second Lieutenant smiled encouragingly, no doubt waiting for an answer that would be suitably inspirational. It wasn't an emotion shared by his superior, Captain Commander Julien Trémaux but, of course, it wouldn't do for him to display such disloyalty.

"My father was with Flatters at Bir-el-Garama," Trémaux said simply while gripping the side of the coach firmly as it shook and rattled over the cobbled passage that led away from the Chateau du Boisselot where the award ceremony had just taken place.

His second-in-command, Luc Girons, a mere 'garçon' in comparison to the much more experienced Trémaux, looked confused. "A bit before my time, sir. Did we teach the damned natives a lesson?"

Trémaux wished he'd kept silent. No-one in France wanted to hear about Bir-el-Girama - not then, not now: it was one of those subjects the expression 'least said, soonest forgotten' was intended for. "No," he said finally, taking off his green cloth képi bearing the hallmark metal hunting horn of the Chasseurs Forestier, the Forest Hunters.

4

An awkward silence hung for a moment and all that could be heard was the coach driver's occasional clipped words of encouragement for the specially-chosen ceremonial chestnut geldings with their flowing white manes. Not that anyone could see them on this cold and dark December night. Algeria seemed so far away that it might as well be on another world. "What happened sir?" Girons persisted. Why wouldn't the man just be quiet? "If you don't mind me asking, of course."

He did mind but refusing to answer would probably only make it worse. "It was the biggest caravan to pass through the desert - nearly 300 animals plus sharpshooters, guides - all the usual paraphernalia. They were scouting out a new railway link between Algeria, the Sudan and Senegal and they ended up being five days with no water and very little sleep."

Trémaux paused for a moment. He'd not really known his father but, for some reason, the loss pained him. "The guides upped and ran off and, a few moments later, 300 Tuareg swept down the side of the Hoggar, out of the sun and with their scimitars and spears jabbing forward. They killed Flatters' troops to a man. Slaughtered every last man Jack of them."

Girons didn't know what to say. What did one say in a world where the expression of emotions was strictly frowned upon? "Sorry, sir. I wasn't aware."

"It was almost exactly thirteen years ago - 16th February 1881. My mother never got over it. I don't think they gave her much by way of detail; after all, it's not exactly something that France is proud of."

Such earnestness was unusual between a Captain Commander and his Lieutenant and neither really knew how to continue the conversation.

It was some time later before Girons felt able to speak again. "What did you think of the Division General, sir? I'd not seen him before although I do believe he once visited our Academy School when I was a cadet." Girons made it sound like he'd been in the army for most of his life instead of just a few years. His youthful tone caused Trémaux to feel particularly ancient although it could just have been the cold night air chilling his bones.

Trémaux didn't dare say what he truly thought - that the whole thing was a sham, a token reward for having given up the best years of his life in the service of La Belle France. "I believe him to be a courageous man," he eventually replied after apparently much consideration. In truth, he just wanted to return to a world he understood and it was a long journey back to Algeria.

"Do you think we'll be seeing any action soon, sir?" Girons persisted. Outside the window, the world continued about its dreary business, seemingly unaware of their little capsule that was hurtling through it. For a moment he wondered which was more real - the frenetic lives of ordinary people whose existence was fraught with the serious routine of surviving, or appeasing the generals and colonels who were obsessed with the ownership of miles of empty sand dunes.

Trémaux had given his youth working his way up through the ranks of the chasseurs. For most, having had a father die in active military service would have been an advantage - a guaranteed introduction to the old boys' club that decided who was suitable material for the upper echelons. Unfortunately for Trémaux, his father was one of the disgraced, an anti-hero whose name was never mentioned in polite conversation as if it were somehow his fault that a bunch of illiterate natives had wiped out a whole expedition of elite French soldiers.

"There's always another battle," he replied eventually.

Yes, there was always another one ready to be fought. Every time some newspaper journalist wrote a story saying about how wars were a thing of the past, a general would stubbornly decide to prove him wrong. Trouble was, Trémaux didn't know any other line of work.

"Will you stay in the army, do you think, sir? I couldn't conceive of doing anything else now."

An idea had gradually been forming inside Trémaux's mind for some time now. It had started back in Algeria when he'd been out with some of the men, celebrating a birthday in true regiment fashion. Two soldiers from the Legion of the Damned, the Foreign Legion, had arrived in their trademark white pantalons and blue serge jackets. They had a strange accent which was hard to place and just kept themselves to themselves in a dignified way which Trémaux quietly envied. "I think you have put your finger on it, Girons," he replied. Girons misunderstood the point which his superior was making and persisted. "I don't plan on settling down," he burbled, "there's too much world to see." At that point the coach hit a rut and skidded sideways, throwing the two men together in the dark. "Sorry, sir," Girons muttered as he straightened himself up.

Yes, for a moment, there was no significant difference between the two men. Rank didn't matter, nothing mattered when you were falling - just like the men he'd killed in battle had fallen. Death, the great leveller. Did the desert recognize the dust which had been his father over the dust which had been the Tuareg whom he'd managed to kill before being gutted by their spears?

"No matter," Trémaux reassured him.

"You dropped your medal, sir," Girons picked up the leather case holding the prestigious object.

Trémaux went to accept it then suddenly stopped, his hand a few centimetres from Girons' own outstretched hand which was holding the medal. "You keep it," he said quietly, pushing it back towards an extremely puzzled Girons.

He wouldn't be needing it where he was bound. As soon as the coach passed Nîmes, he was going to disembark and sign up with the Legion.

Why?

Have you ever wondered about how the 'Keep Off The Grass' signs get where they are or how the grass that you're supposed to keep off is ever mown? Do you think about why they only lend money to people who don't want it and tell those who do to get stuffed? Does it seem in the slightest bit logical that a chunk of our taxes goes towards paying for one bunch of people to save lives and to another bunch to end them prematurely? Tell me, why do you have to be crazy to think that the insane is actually sane?

That particular morning, these were some of the questions that were battering away at the inside of my skull just like a stream of ricocheting bullets. At least they would have put me out of my misery. Instead the insistent thoughts gave me a violent headache with which I was still expected to execute the million-and-one banal functions of a humdrum life with the perfect precision demanded of me as a responsible member of society.

And there's another thing. What am I supposed to be responsible for and why aren't I being trained and properly remunerated for holding down such a responsible position?

I briefly contemplated the idea of discussing my philosophical dilemma with my wife but I think the last time we talked about anything important was the day we made our vows and that was so long ago that I seem to remember we had to sign in copperplate. I had no justifiable cause for giving her a cardiac infarction so, in the manner of our relationship, I said absolutely nothing. I just waved her goodbye in the usual absent-minded way, got into my car, and drove to the office. As always, the traffic was bad with everyone trying to get to much the same place at much the same time. Why? Why in all that purported to be sane did we have roads that were bigger than strictly necessary in order to accommodate traffic that was worse than it needed to be? I gazed with envy at the empty bus lane. Bus lane? There was a joke. Environmentally friendly? That was another one. Try waiting at a stop for a bus that doesn't come or, if it does, has an engine which is wheezing diesel fumes like an old rheumy who can't afford meths and is so overcrowded the gropers are fighting for 'lebensraum'.

I usually drive in silence - choosing to be alone with my depressing thoughts. Today, however, I decided that I just couldn't stand the noise in my head a second longer. Put on the radio, I told myself. Kill the silence, I said. The traffic-lights were on red while my fellow motorists and I waited for non-existent cars to turn out of a street that virtually no-one ever went down because most of the businesses along it had gone bust after someone decided it was OK if they took all of the pie while others had nothing.

My default station is the one which plays classical music. OK, the frequent advert breaks are more than a bit irritating but the music itself is soothing and familiar. Today, though, I didn't want familiar; I wanted change. But is change merely an abnormality that becomes the normality if we keep choosing it? Plus ça change, plus c'est la même chose, the French say. The more it changes, the more it stays the same. What the hell, I thought, why don't I live on the edge a bit? That's why I found a hard rock station and was merrily doing my best headbanger impersonation until a woman pushing a pram knocked on my car window to inquire if I was having some kind of fit.

I managed to refrain from saying that her baby had a face that looked like she'd stuck the nappy on the wrong end. That's because all babies are beautiful, aren't they? It's written that we must compliment someone for successfully dumping yet another screaming brat onto an already overcrowded planet. Convention demands it. In the end, I just reassured her that I was minding my own business and enjoying singing along to one of my favourite hits - I want to hear your bones crack as performed by Act of Violence. That got rid of her.

I so desperately wanted to swing out of the lane I was in, drive along in the empty bus one to my left or use the right-turn lane that was on the green filter but I didn't. I stuck responsibly to where I was supposed to be and, as a result, arrived at the office a good fifteen minutes late. What's 'good' about something bad? Have you ever asked yourself that? No, probably not. Very wise.

By the time that I'd pulled into the car park, it'd started to rain. There's something about rain in November - it seems to penetrate anything and everything you wear. It's cold and damp, far more so than rain in the other winter months, and not something you want to be soaked in while you perform the battery of meaningless tasks that your employer sees fit to burden you with.

Anyway, there were two empty spaces within a distance that didn't entail taking too much of an ice-cold shower. One was for ordinary employees like me, the hive's drones, and the other was for the Queen Bee himself. He'd buzzed off on an exotic holiday - no waiting until Christmas in order to snatch a couple of Statutory Days for him, oh no; so, because he was working hard at getting an unseasonable melanoma, his space was free. You couldn't park in it, though. Not a chance. Not if you didn't want a half-hour lecture from his secretary - that's if she could find sufficient words in her limited repertoire. Two more jokes for you - she never has time for anything if you ask her to do something and the other is that she's hardly a secretary because she can't help herself from blabbing the company's private business to all and sundry.

Apart from having unfeasibly large hooters and possessing a penchant for wearing skirts that don't seem to go below the level of her belt, I can't think why the boss chose her. Put it this way, I don't think there's a male in the building who couldn't tell you whether she's wearing the knickers with the jocular keyhole on them or the other pair she seems to wear from time to time with the big 'No-Entry' sign printed on the front and 'Keep Out' on the back.

Isn't life just one big bowl of cherries?

To return to the matter of the car park, there was the other space.

By the way, have you ever wondered why a space ceases to be a space just because there's something occupying a part of it? How much space does there have to be before it reaches criticality? Does it cease to be a space while an object is moving into it or does it have to wait until the object is stationary?

Anyway, it was actually two parking spaces which had been transformed into one by the thoughtless parking of our company's resident dickhead also known as my line manager. He'd made it to the rarefied height of Chief Nonentity by keeping a log of every personal call - incoming and outgoing - that his predecessor had received or made. After a few months, he handed the diary to the Big Boss - the one with the secretary of not-so-hidden charms. You can guess the rest. Time for a reshuffle and a new appointment, "Rise, Sir Dickhead". The ugly deed was done.

Anyway, I had to park about as far from the front door as was possible. It was fast approaching the point where it would have been easier for me to have left the car at home and walked in. By the time I got under cover, I was shivering with cold and soaked to the skin. Another day in paradise had well and truly begun.

The receptionist - she's a pert-looking creature with auburn hair done in a severely tight bun, large green-framed glasses and a turquoise blouse - an attempt at colour co-ordination, perhaps - gave me a sour look of welcome before picking up the phone and smiling warmly at the caller who unfortunately, of course, didn't have an opportunity to bask in her affections. Something was welling up inside me: I had this overwhelming urge to be different. I can't explain why - I just did. As a result, I took off my tie - the one with the company logo that we're all supposed to wear to destruction; even when it's still bearing signs of the greasy barbecue chicken wings that, along with some stale crisps, constituted the office party beanfeast. I also decided to walk up the stairs rather than use the lift. I was a true rebel!

I imagined the effect I'd have if I roared into the car park one morning, clad in leathers and astride a Harley Davidson complete with chromed ape-hangers and a busty topless chick hanging on behind me - just like a poster I used to have in my study at school. The warmth of the thought even counteracted some of the cold I was feeling and, just for once, I actually managed to feel some affinity with my work.

While on my way to my desk, I was waylaid by none less than Sir Dickhead himself. Where've you been, he demanded - right in front of the office junior, a vacuous and adenoidal individual who looked like he'd be better suited signing up as a guinea pig for a skincare pharmaceutical. Do you know what time it is? He spat the question at me while I contemplated asking him which time zone or even which calendar system he was referring to.

Apparently my tardiness was costing the company a small fortune. If it's a fortune, how can it be small? Surely that's a contradiction in terms? I wanted desperately to tell him that I'd have been five minutes earlier if I'd not had to park miles away because some inconsiderate twat not a million miles away - he was actually only a few inches from me - had parked boss-eyed across the last two spaces in the bloody car park. However, I didn't. I said nothing. I just kept my thoughts to myself like I always did.

I think that he soon realised that he wasn't going to get a rise - no way would I give that clown the satisfaction of seeing that he was getting to me - and decided to move on to much more weighty matters such as when to send out a memo about not wasting paper or going on a campaign such as 'a tidy desk is a tidy mind'. Whatever it was, you could be sure that it would be utterly pointless.

Was his job something to aspire to - even though, of course, I had no chance of getting there? I've got no drive, apparently. Anyway, that's what Sir Dickhead told me at my last employee evaluation. Let me paraphrase that such sessions are fifteen minutes of fame that you don't want unless you happen to enjoy cringing. You get to listen to a diatribe of the things that you should or could have done if only you'd possessed the gift of clairvoyancy. With his own combination of 20/20 hindsight and 'Don't talk before, during or after my rant' attitude, there was nothing to do but contemplate the dubious joy of knowing that some other poor sod would be sitting precisely where you were not long hence.

So, I'd had a dose of being treated like a naughty boy who'd handed in his homework after the deadline. Had he ever criticised me for being a bit late leaving? No, of course not, because he was almost always the first to go, that's why! Save, naturally, for when the Big Boss was doing his rounds: at those times you'd see him suddenly get a load of files out of the cabinet and appear to be poring over them. I'd even heard him say things like 'Got to find a way of cutting those overheads, sir' and 'Delegation? No, sir, I want the job done properly'. It didn't matter if the files he had grabbed related to employees who'd had the wit to leave years earlier or if they were stuffed full of his pointless memos, it must have looked impressive even if it wasn't.

Ten minutes later and I was at my desk - my refuge, save that it wasn't of course. My colleagues - I can't call them workmates because they neither do much by way of work nor are they 'mates' - gave their usual assortment of grunted greetings and looks of contempt before returning to their own grey and humdrum existence.

It was while I was busy fending off calls asking for things that hadn't arrived but which should have arrived if someone else had done something or other as they were supposed to, and also untangling the paperclip chain that our witty - why do you call someone 'witty' when they are clearly witless - junior had thought to be an hilarious wheeze, that I decided enough was enough this time.

Perhaps it was the splendid view of the puddles in the company car park that my office window afforded me, or perhaps it was the exciting knowledge that, in the space of a few short hours - are there long ones - I would be able to go home, not discuss with my ever-loving wife just precisely what I'd not done all day at work, and then go to bed, get up and do it all over again, that changed something inside of me.

For some reason, I don't know what precisely, the dread that I'd normally feel about how my whole existence defined the word 'tedious', had completely disappeared. I was no longer bored or frustrated, I was instead suddenly filled with a lightness of spirit, a feeling that anything and everything was within my grasp. I was destined to be someone after all.

The morning flew by as I contemplated how I should best strike a blow for freedom and become the guy who places the 'Keep off' signs - in a metaphorical sense, of course. I would be the one who sets the rules, decides who, when, how and where. The thought was intoxicating - completely so - and I even laughed to myself about getting breathalysed while under the influence of being a man or even a human once again. Yes, Officer, I have had a little whiff of what I could be if only ...

I wondered if any of the other drones around me ever had such original thoughts or had they been so thoroughly lobotomised that it was no longer possible for them to contemplate anything other than keeping to the straight and narrow? Banality should be a recognised illness. Doctors, take note!

Well, plus ça change, plus ça change would be my motto henceforth. I couldn't wait to explain the good news to my wife. Which would confound her more - the fact that I'd evolved or the fact that I'd chosen to speak to her about something that actually mattered?

Anyway, there was important work to do in the office first and the end of the morning was rapidly approaching. The rain had stopped, too - surely that was a good sign? I looked at my car; it was grey-blue in colour, just like my life had become. Time to go for Ferrari red or British Racing Green? Anything was possible if you put your mind to it.

I was so excited that I think I muttered something about 'bringing something back for everyone' as I left but I can't be completely sure about that now. I do know that I literally raced down the stairs and over to my car with a speed that I'd not felt possible in many of those long years I mentioned earlier. There you have it.

So, that's why I went to the ironmongers' at lunchtime and that's why I did what I did afterwards, OK? That's enough for now. My time is far too valuable so just don't ask me again because I've nothing more to say until my lawyer gets here, and if you still haven't got it, for goodness sake don't ask me 'why?'

Time is of the essence

We arrange to meet - he with total conviction that the event will take place as planned, me utterly resigned to yet another no-show.

The time arrives and there's no sign of him. I'm there, like I always am, ready and waiting patiently as I always do. But, of course, there's something much more important that's distracted him and diverted him from our assignation.

When we meet next, I remind him of the missed appointment; he just shrugs it off in his usual casual manner.

"Do you know what a flake is?" I ask, irritated by his dismissive attitude.

"You mean, am I a chip off the old block?" he jokes.

"No," I snap, "it's someone who's inherently unreliable, someone who bails out on his appointments."

He sneers, "I'm paying you a small fortune for these sessions."

"Yes," I reply, "but you need to actually attend them in order to improve."

Perception

I am your companion, sometimes large, sometimes small.

You make faces at me and I poke faces back at you.

I don't ever lie but you stick your tongue out at me anyway and I always return the compliment.

When you cry, so do I, but I don't ever even attempt to comfort you.

Does all this make me less than human? Yes, by your rules.

I'm often accused of flattery, or slander, or even both, but only because of your designated perception.

It's not in my character to exaggerate, or to minimise, not unless I happen to be warped, or cracked.

I'm not your friend and I'm not your enemy, although if you break me I'm sharp enough to slit your throat.

Then you'd avoid the seven years of bad luck I'd bring you; that sort of twist suits my dark sense of humour.

Sticks & stones

The racket was phenomenal. Even from well over fifty yards away, Hugh could see that his stone had put a nice round dent in the rusty corrugated iron wall of the outside privy. He deftly pocketed his sportsman's catapult and ducked into the undergrowth for fear of reprisals for his action.

"I knows it were you, you little bass-tard!" came the outraged cry from old Mr Williams as he emerged from the privy shaking his fist in anger. His braces were dangling from his scrawny shoulders and his shirt-tail hung over his brown corduroy working man's trousers.

But a boy had to practise somehow and somewhere. Catapult practice was something Hugh always took very seriously because he needed to. He was just one boy on his own pitched up against a whole gang of boys: thin, gormless, tufty-haired, vicious kids with catapults of their own and a violent, moronic leader called Ray who took great delight in orchestrating sadistic acts.

Hugh had been hounded for as far back as he could remember for his size, which was none of his choosing: Fatty, Piggy, Porky, Lardy, Dough-boy, they called him - behind his back, to his face and in front of others. He was forever being the odd-one-out, the misfit that the primitive instincts in his peers automatically excluded from their herd. On just about every school exercise book he had ever possessed, the last letter of his Christian name had been changed to an 'e' - Huge Bennett - hilarious.

Worse still was an incident that had occurred a few weeks back. A drawing pin had been left on his chair, its point upwards, ostensibly to see if he would go 'pop' when he sat on it. In fact its point went straight into one of his testicles - something which caused him to yelp with pain, much to the anger of his teacher. "Sit still and shut up, Hugh!" he'd snapped. Save that he'd deliberately drawn out the single syllable of the name to make it a close match for 'Huge' - an act duly recognised and appreciated by the regular gang of tormentors. Of course, there was no action taken against the boy who'd placed the pin there in the first place - just humiliation for Hugh who had dared to protest.

Forget school, the main lesson he was learning was the law of the jungle. In essence, it was no good depending upon others to do the right thing - you need to learn to depend upon your own ability to prevent the wrong thing from occurring. Being 'prickly' Hugh called it.

It wasn't just one teacher either - it had become commonplace for the others to exclude him from activities with an array of sarcastic and supposedly humorous remarks, playing to a delighted gallery. One of the good old standards that the more feeble of these teachers fell back on was to imply that he was too slow-witted to react in time. And this was the boy who'd finished reading the whole series of school readers by the age of 8, but then of course that was simply an irrelevance, a fluke, a bagatelle.

Lessons were bad but playtimes were much, much worse. He'd recently seen another fat boy reduced to a snivelling and bloody pulp in the school playground but then this was a boy who never posed any physical threat in return - he was just a victim, pure and simple.

Somehow he sensed that his enemies would not stop short of his annihilation and there was definitely no superhero coming to protect him from them.

Talk to his parents? Well, parent, to be precise. He'd tried to act maturely and discuss the bullying with his divorced mother but all she did was to lecture him about the need to make friends (which she'd had no problems doing when she was a girl) and how he mustn't upset her own current friends. These grown-up women were the girls she'd grown up with and now the mothers of the kids who were terrorising him. Through her blinkered eyes, it was all a case of him needing to 'fit in' and to knuckle down at school and not antagonise the teachers. They were only trying to do a job which he was making all the more difficult with his attitude and behaviour.

It was all a lost cause for Hugh so, for this reason, he'd spent hours customising his catapult: transforming a simple fisherman's casting device into a weapon of power and deadly accuracy. It was now far superior to any that could be bought in a shop.

He'd got it in the first place by feigning an interest in fishing and protesting that his lack of strength prevented him from casting the bait to any distance. The confession caused the salesman to regard him with a look of absolute disgust, but conveniently distracted him from asking awkward questions about its real intended use.

When he got home, Hugh retained the original frame, but discarded the feeble, all-in-one rubber strip and pouch that had accompanied the catapult in favour of two long, sturdy strips of rubber and a pouch made from the tongue of an old leather shoe which he'd bought at a village jumble sale. He then spent hours calibrating the contraption, after first having carefully filed off all of the roughness from the alloy frame, and greased the rubber at the points where it passed through the holes in the metal.

He was just as precise about his choice of ammunition which was clean, rounded limestone scalpings that he always scooped up from the electricity substation. These stones were the best - they flew the furthest and they were the most accurate.

Hugh had just used up one of these precious missiles on Mr Williams' privy - a little light-hearted indulgence he permitted himself now and then. The man was a well-known miserable old git and the sight of him going into his outside toilet and closing the door behind him was just too enticing. Let him undo his braces, sit down, open his paper, wait two minutes and then fire!

However Hugh had plenty more ammunition in the lining of his coat, the place where it ended up after it had dropped through the holes in his pockets. His coats were always getting worn out pockets-first - something which, when his mother discovered it or he needed to ask for a replacement coat, prompted her to subject him to an earful of how much his extra-large clothes cost her. Didn't he know how hard she had to work for her money?

Today he was heading, via the paddock behind Mr Williams' garden, for the Upper Woods, an area of mixed and mature woodland just about visible from the village as a dark mass on the horizon. It looked as if it was about to rain, but then rain might well mean that the boys he feared would hang around closer to home, or even stay indoors, thus leaving him able to roam in peace and relative security. He had to get out of his own tiny house from time to time or face going stir-crazy.

Once in the wood, he made straight for his favourite spot, a steep chalky mound in the middle of an area of dense undergrowth. Exposed tree roots made crude steps by which he could climb up to sit behind the hollowed-out remains of a tree that had long since fallen. There was a wonderful odour of pine-needles and leaf-mould and it was his own citadel, a place which he'd defended successfully from attackers on several previous occasions.

Sitting with his eyes closed, relishing the first drops of rain on his upturned face, he heard the explosive alarm call of a blackbird back in the direction from which he'd just come. It might not have been anything, though: blackbirds had plenty of other reasons for being startled. But he sat with his eyes open now, his pulse quickening.

There was an eerie silence for some minutes and then, quite close at hand, a wren started chattering angrily and a small twig snapped. Hugh ducked behind the tree trunk and slowly, carefully, so as not to make a sound, extracted a handful of stones from his coat and placed them on the ground to his left. His heartbeat was pounding in his ears, making it difficult for him to hear anything else.

Another eternity passed. All of a sudden there was a sound behind him: the sort of popping noise that is made by someone squatting down in Wellington boots. He spun round and peered into the undergrowth at the foot of the mound but there was nothing to be seen. That didn't mean that there was nothing there - by now he was sure he was not alone. How many were there? Who were they? What did they intend to do?

Then, out of the corner of his eye, he saw a movement: someone had just slipped behind the trunk of a tree. This was in front of him, so whoever these kids were, they were trying to surround him.

He could hear more movements, now: stealthy footsteps in all different directions. He slipped a stone into the pouch of his catapult, took up the slack with his left arm and peered round, ready to fire.

Something caught his eye. It was long and thin, like a stick, and it was poking out from behind a tree which he knew to be a mere fifteen yards away. The stick slid forward like a stiff snake, and he realised, at the same moment, that behind it was Ray – the tufty hair was unmistakeable. What Hugh could see, pointing straight at his head, was the barrel of an air-rifle - probably just a .177 but still capable of maiming him.

Realising that his choice was limited to a simple binary 'hurt or get hurt' decision, Hugh acted with the smooth efficiency of the well-practised and the totally committed. He pulled back the pouch of his catapult to the full extent of the rubber strips, quickly aimed, and let loose. The sudden release of energy caused the stone to fly through the air towards its target – whatever was behind the gun barrel.

There was a whistling noise - usually all that was needed to send his enemies scuttling for cover - and then a dull thud and a high-pitched scream. The next thing he saw was Ray standing clear of the tree, no longer holding the gun but with one hand clapped to his right eye while blood gushed out from between his clenched fingers.

Hugh's arms fell by his sides. That was it, now, there was no going back, there could be no question of claiming it was an accident. Ray would be the victim, the one wronged, and Hugh would be expected to pay dearly. Everyone would have deaf ears for his account of what had happened just like they always did. He knew from repeated bitter experiences that there would be no space for the truth - if a story didn't fit, it needed to be made to. It wouldn't be the first time that he'd got into trouble for defending himself and he suspected that this time his life as he knew it would be over. No-one would stand up for him, least of all his mother. Borstal was the usual destiny for delinquents such as he'd suddenly become, and there his very existence would be under threat every single day.

An eye for a life; a life for an eye. Hardly a fair exchange. But there was defiance and even triumph in Hugh's own eyes as he carefully poked his catapult into a hidden crevice in the tree trunk.

Unlucky for some

There's no-one sitting in seat number 7. They've left it empty on purpose - in honour of the dead. Not that the boy who would have occupied it was honoured very much when he was alive but then that's the way of schools, isn't it? It's all about appearances and what has to be seen to be done. That's why there's an empty seat in our examination room.

I wasn't exactly what you'd call pally with Daniels - the boy who would have occupied the empty chair in question. He was an odd sort of kid - physically, mentally and socially. You'd see him in class, blatantly in a world of his own and presenting a direct challenge to the teacher concerning the focal point of his attention. On the sports pitch, he was more of an obstacle than a player - someone you tried hard to avoid picking or, if you were unfortunate enough to have him on your team, the player you always tried to steer the action as far away as possible from.

Socially, he was a complete disaster. At break-time, he'd be sitting on his own, peering through his chipped bottle-bottom glasses at his crustless, gluten-free sandwiches and his special extra-bioactive yoghurt until one of the older boys decided to see how high they could propel it out of his hands. If he felt anything, he didn't show it - just understood that it was destined to happen with a kind of bovine acceptance.

Bullying. Yep, bullying is an intrinsic part of our school activities. If you can't beat them on your own, join in with someone bigger who can - that's how it goes. That's the school's unspoken motto.

Bullying may be a fact of life but, in my humble opinion - to coin a phrase - its existence should not be broadened to encompass hostilities conducted by teachers. No sir, in my book such actions are quite out of order and that's how I came to form a kind of association with Daniels. I certainly wouldn't have done so otherwise.

Anyway, this is the story as he told me.

Like I said, Daniels wasn't the sharpest knife in the box which explains why our chemistry teacher was forever exasperated by his poor performance. Then, again, he must have been equally frustrated by the complete refusal of the Back Row Brigade to pay even the vaguest bit of attention to anything he was saying. Of course, the Back Row Brigade were also known for two other things – firstly they were big ugly bastards who collectively would have fancied their chances against a lone teacher and secondly their fathers had considerable capital behind them. Attacking them verbally in any serious way would start a chain reaction that was pretty much guaranteed to end up with the chemistry teacher sitting in the headmaster's office getting some major earache about how he needed to review his teaching methods.

That left Daniels. As far as I could figure, he was from a one-parent family - only his mother ever turned up for those horribly embarrassing parents' evenings when teachers feign interest in kids they either don't remember or would rather forget and parents selectively hear how their dim-witted offspring is doing 'rather well'. That sentiment applies even if 'rather well' is tantamount to saying 'not as bad as we'd dreaded'.

Daniels' mother was a fey blonde-haired creature who always made me think of one of the elves in Lord of the Rings. I doubt someone like her could have conceived of the regimented cruelty a public school like ours can provide - especially for kids like her son who had 'Victim' emblazoned through him like a stick of rock at the seaside.

Anyway, bullying was one thing but teachers doing it too was a no-no in my books. That's why I was prepared to come to Daniels' assistance when he'd had a particularly rough time with the chemistry teacher and was facing an even worse one when he handed in his homework. We'd been set the job of balancing some chemical reaction equations - thus combining chemistry and mathematics - two subjects which Daniels was particularly unsuited to and which unfortunately just happened to be taught by the same brutal bastard.

We'd been paired up to do an experiment which meant that I had to put him in charge of watching the tap drip while I did the work otherwise I'd be in much the same boat as him when

I came to write up the results. That's when I offered to help him with his homework on the strict condition that he deliberately got a few answers wrong just to make it look convincing.

That didn't make us friends, soul-mates or long-lost brothers. It was just me thumbing my nose at the system and wanting to avoid having to listen to the chemistry teacher's rant about how bizarre it was that the great evolutionary force combined with n-quadrillion carbon atoms could manage to produce such an abortion as Daniels.

Then came the mid-year exams - the mocks before the real exams that summer which is where I am right now. Yes, I'm in the middle of an exam and this is going to form part of my papers.

Is it an English exam? No, it's my first chemistry paper. What the ... ? I hear you ask - well, I would hear you if we were together, I'm sure.

Let me explain by back-tracking a moment.

Anyway, there was Daniels, sitting in seat number 7 staring blankly at his chemistry paper. Suddenly he started writing at such a speed I thought his pen was going to catch fire in his hand. Well, OK, that's a touch of hyperbole but it's not much of an exaggeration - the boy was absolutely on fire.

It was the same for all of the exams. He came in, sat down, began writing and was finished in roughly half of the time that we'd been allocated. At the beginning, the invigilators wouldn't let him leave his seat but word soon went around that he'd clearly done all of the required questions, and provided he left the hall with a minimum of commotion, he was free to leave. He couldn't return of course, but he made no effort to so that was fair enough.

Then all hell broke loose. It turned out that he'd got just about full marks for every question on every paper. If the class creep had done that, they'd have been suspicious but Daniels? There was no way in our hallowed halls that such a blasphemous thing could happen, could it?

He was immediately summoned to the headmaster's office where he was asked to account for his high marks. I don't know what he said but clearly it didn't satisfy the Exalted One. As a result, his mother was firmly invited to attend but I doubt she had much idea about anything and I suspect she merely muddied the waters by her presence.

With Daniels sticking rigidly to his story that he hadn't smuggled in his textbooks (books which he'd never been able to make sense of in class), there was only one solution - he must have seen the papers in advance. But they'd been kept in the school safe, accessible only to the headmaster and the deputy head. The finger of suspicion pointed from one potential culprit to another as if it were the clicker on a lottery wheel.

Anyway, try as they might, they couldn't break Daniels' protests of innocence nor could they find any hint of incriminating evidence. They searched his books locker, his sports locker, the contents of his phone; they asked his mother to search his home and even to bring in his laptop. There was nothing - zero. With great reluctance and the utmost ill-grace on the part of the school, Daniels was accorded pole position in all subjects. Some teachers took the news better than others.

Just about the bottom of the list for graceful acceptance was, of course, our friendly chemistry and mathematics teacher. While he couldn't or didn't dare make allegations that clearly couldn't be substantiated about Daniels' exam mark, he had to content himself by stirring up trouble for the boy. As a result, we were subjected to a barrage of awful puns such as:

"Don't cheat with the results"

"Put the magnesium in the crib"

"No just copying what it says in the book"

Along with unsubtle remarks like:

"Daniels, show me your hands and arms"

"Daniels, I'm watching you"

"Daniels, you'll tell me if I get something wrong, won't you?"

And just because he didn't dare make accusations, it didn't mean others couldn't. Pretty soon even the single brain-celled Back Row Brigade had twigged on the advantages to be afforded by bullying Daniels into letting them in on his little secret. When he stuck to his story that there was no secret, that just sent them the message that their particular brand of cruelty wasn't vindictive enough. Time to step it up a gear. Sure enough the violence increased. Beatings were conducted with ruthless thoroughness on a more or less daily basis and it was rare to see Daniels without blood-splattered clothes or a plaster or two carelessly stuck on by our bored and myopic matron.

It would have been little good him approaching any of the teachers. For starters, one didn't simply complain about such things, old chap - they're character-building, damnation. Secondly, I doubt many of the teachers disapproved of the retribution which they were doubtless vicariously participating in.

Maybe I could have spoken up. Maybe I might have made a small difference if I'd shouted "That's enough!!!" but I didn't. I neither condoned nor did I condemn: I neither prevented nor participated in what was taking place. While I make no excuses for my inaction - I shall live with that shame - I doubt there really was anything that I could have done that would have made a positive difference.

If Daniels had been reclusive and remote before, he was even more so now. He wandered from one classroom to the next, receiving the customary kicks, thumps, pokes, prods and incessant verbal abuse with absolute passivity. I suspect that he had withdrawn to some inner place where he didn't feel the pain in the same way as he would have done otherwise.

The last time I spoke to Daniels, he seemed to have perked up considerably - so much so that he was bursting to talk to me. While dialogue between us had not really ceased, we'd never been what you might call chatty with each other. There was obviously something bothering him and I wondered if he was ready to tell me his secret - he was.

What followed was nearly impossible to believe and I would have given just about any other boy a stroppy punch in the arm for daring to try to take me for such a complete and gullible fool. However, firstly Daniels had never demonstrated any semblance of an over-active imagination, secondly he had the marks to back up his words, and thirdly he didn't look at all to me like he was lying.

I do suspect most of what he said was just plain superstition - the shirt he'd put on back-to-front the morning it all happened, the bus-driver forgetting to punch his ticket - that sort of thing. However he did say something which made as much sense as anything he came out with and that's what I'm putting into practice today.

I wanted to ask Daniels more - especially after I'd tried out his idea in anger but that was not to be. The bullying from his peers and his teachers finally proved too much, and at full-school assembly on the Monday after our little conversation, the headmaster informed us that Daniels, the school's star pupil, had regrettably suffered an accident.

The accident, of course, turned out to be that he'd 'accidentally' put his head through a noose which he'd 'accidentally' tied. Still, it wouldn't do to say the 'suicide' word after a rousing rendition of 'In England's Green and Pleasant Land', would it? No, such words were reserved for the local Comprehensive School's riff-raff and their more plebeian ways of building character in boys.

I spent some time reflecting on what he'd told me: how he'd somehow made contact with a force which couldn't be explained in terms of a mere chemical equation. How he'd raised it in the first place, goodness only knew, but he made it clear that it wasn't like in those silly films where some soon-to-be-slaughtered teenager says 'Supercalifragilisticexpialidocious' three times in a mirror and then gets beaten to death by an umbrella-wielding madwoman.

Anyway, I felt confident that I could handle the benefits of his secret in a more responsible and less obvious way than Daniels and that's why I'm following his instructions to the letter.

He told me that in order to summon the force, it'd said all he needed to do was to write 'There's no-one sitting in seat number 7' at the beginning of his first paper, so that's what I've done today.

The end

I'm writing this because I've literally no choice and there's also nothing else to do. It started a few weeks back. No, let me rewind a moment. I'm an author although given the confused beginning you'd be excused for thinking otherwise. Anyway, I ghost-wrote a book about hacking for a regular client. He was enthusiastic about the work and asked me to include some actual case studies, which I did.

The trouble is I maligned a hacker. I suggested he or she - we've never been formally introduced - was less than competent. My customer then published the book, and having been paid for my services, I started on a new project for another client.

This morning we were late getting up because none of the alarm clocks went off. That was just the beginning. Our toaster didn't work, the dishwasher hadn't washed the mugs and dinner things from last night, and you try getting the kids off for school when the doors and windows have been locked down by an unresponsive security system. I couldn't even boil a kettle. I put the television on to see if we'd had one of those solar flares - just a blue screen. And the radio won't budge from the evangelical channel. The kids aren't amused - they want their pop music back.

Telephone for help? Do you think I haven't tried? There's no hint of a signal and there's no internet service save for this one site which I've been allowed to access and where I'm now posting my apology.

Let me be very clear. You have an exceptionally rare talent and this is evident from the horrible pickle you've put me in today.

So, there you go, that's my sincerest apology. Please will you kindly open my front door now?

A part of the deal

Mummy! Daddy! Please don't fight," Marvin, my three-year-old son begged while limpet-like grabbing first my wife's dress and then my best navy blue trousers I'd just got back from the dry-cleaners. They really didn't need his greasy paw-prints - I had an important meeting the next day and I was intending to wear them.

My wife knew damned well I liked to be left alone when I got home which meant both her and the kid were supposed to be out of sight, out of mind, and dead bloody silent while I calmed down - that was the deal. They'd no idea what it's like working in the city as a contract negotiator for a specialist management consultancy. We get called in by the big companies - those typically looking to land a major construction project, win a lease for development of natural resources, or secure some international defence deal to supply weapon systems. Anyway, I come home shagged out every night and I just require peace and quiet. Am I asking too much?

I didn't mean what happened next. I was just frustrated, fractious and generally exasperated. What did she expect? Anyway ...

"Get off me, you stupid little sod," I shouted, swatting Marvin away like the persistent and irritating fly he was emulating. Why couldn't the silly cow keep him under control? She had all day to instil some discipline into him so what the hell was she doing with her time? I'm not some kind of animal and I really didn't mean to knock him hard; I must've caught him just-so on the side of his head. Anyway, it sent him backwards against an antique three-legged occasional table which I'd spent a fortune on getting restored. Both him and the table went flying, along with a lead crystal vase which landed on his arm making him screech. Luckily it didn't break.

The subsequent noise was like someone grinding steel - and then my wife joined in with her own brand of yuppyville affected blubbing. It was more than anyone could stand.

I'm a bit hazy about what happened afterwards. They say she attacked me with one arm while grabbing Marvin with the other. Who knows? Anyway, she ended up with a shiner and I ended up sitting in this tribunal room where I am now.

"Mr Williams, are you listening to me?" the magistrate droned. He was a nondescript kind of man, the sort you'd never normally notice who probably hung around in the municipal golf course bar dreaming of a cordially-worded invite to play at one of the more exclusive links. It was an invitation which, of course, would never be forthcoming. Anyway, he had a drawn face with sunken eyes and a hint of a dental scar on the right-hand side of his jaw.

"Yes, of course I'm listening," I said glancing overtly at my Breitling watch that had probably cost as much as the ugly little man in front of me got paid in six months. "I don't have a lot of choice, do I?"

"That's exactly what you do have, Mr Williams, as I've been trying to explain. You were fortunate this time in that ... uh ... Marvin wasn't seriously injured however such experiences can easily traumatise young minds. You've heard the report from Social Services recommending prosecution? Well, what do you say? Do you want to try this new behaviour modification programme or do you want to risk going to prison?"

I nearly told him where to go and what to do when he got there but realised it was just what he wanted. Come on, Vernon, I told myself, this is only another negotiation situation.

"Look, I had a really bad day. How about I take him to Disneyland to make up and promise never to do it again?"

Before the judge could respond, my wife, Marilyn, jumped in.

"If you don't do this thing they're offering you, Vernon, I'll press charges, sue for divorce, claim sole custody of Marvin, and clean you out financially." She said the words with a surprising amount of passion and conviction but there was a cold undertone to it.

I was gobsmacked; well, I'd never have thought the girl had it in her. Somehow she must have found some spine underneath all that ghastly make-up she plasters herself with. Whatever next? Ask me to get my own dinner while she paints her toe-nails?

"Well, Mr Williams? Your wife has made her position abundantly clear. Do you wish to take your chance in court or will you accept entry onto the programme? Please don't waste all of our time suggesting some preposterous third option because I have other cases this afternoon so ..."

"I'll do it," I said without thinking of the consequences. It was clear I didn't have much by way of bargaining chips - meaning it's time to cut losses and run. Anyway, what was so terrible about playing some silly game with a computer?

The judge coughed. "Mr Williams. You will forgive me for saying this but I'm not convinced you're taking this seriously. Let me make the court's position perfectly clear. If you commence this programme, you must finish it or face having any sentence handed to you significantly increased."

By the way this meeting had gone, I had about as much chance of escaping scot-free as a wet dog turd did of winning 'Fragrance of the Year'. Where was my legal advisor? I'd decided against one as my experience is they only get everything around their necks - although this wasn't exactly going to plan, was it?

"I've had enough of your bullying, Vernon. It's time you stopped, otherwise ... ". My wife's voice trailed off and she returned to her normal tearful self. While it wasn't working on me, it was no surprise to see her well-rehearsed 'Pity me' routine getting the judge's sympathy vote as he obligingly grabbed a box of Kleenex from the top of a filing cabinet.

"Don't worry, Mrs Williams. The programme has had some excellent results."

And that was that. My fate had been sealed and this whole sorry story set in motion. If I'd known ahead about what it'd involve, I'd have probably volunteered right then for 'Hide the Salami' and 'Leapfrog with the Lifers' or whatever other contact-sport games were currently in vogue at Her Majesty's finest long-stay hotels.

I was immediately confined to house arrest courtesy of an ankle bracelet with a charming little traffic light system of LED's on it. Green was if I stayed inside the house. The light changed to amber if I went more than ten metres from the building and red went off along with an alarm at the police station if I strayed further. Red meant 'off to jail' without a sniff at passing via 'Go'.

I'd managed to arrange to work largely from home but there would be no pressing the flesh with clients or their customers - something I'd always found efficacious. I reckon negotiating's like poker. The kids these days prefer playing online but I'd rather 'play the other players' by sitting in front of them and taking advantage of their tells.

A team of workmen blundered around my beautiful home, drilling holes, running cables along wainscoting and wrecking furnishings I had shelled out a not-so-small fortune on. It was hard biting my tongue but I'd been warned - button it or spend the time in jail. Buttoning won.

A week later the system was operational and every room had its Big Brother network of cameras and microphones. Behind it all, locked in a tamper-proof safe was the controlling computer. I had no access to it bar through microphones which if I fiddled with or destroyed would end up with me saying 'howdy-doody' to the nonces and other assorted prison riff-raff.

There was another gadget - a phone that was only capable of dialling one number. Ring it and I'd be let out. If I'd passed the programme, my criminal record would be unblemished but fail and I would be whisked to a court of law with my failure counting against me. Wonderful.

The surly operative who installed the system seemed incapable of stringing an entire sentence together. He was obviously one of these nerdy types who'd probably rather gawp at some doe-eyed manga creature than at a real woman with the best bazookas a Harley Street plastic surgeon could fabricate.

"You're going to star in your own show," he sniggered as he picked up his bag of tools on the final day of the installation. It was the most he'd said.

"Why don't you go and ...," I started but thought better of it. He winked, blew me a kiss, and left before I lost my self control.

I'd scarcely shut the door when a synthesized voice came from everywhere yet nowhere at the same time.

"Just you an' me now, pardner." The computer spoke in a Texan drawl.

"It's just me. You aren't real - in case you'd not noticed."

"Well, ain't that a jim-dandy state of affairs. Can't say I'd realised - much obliged to you. Name's Marty, by the way."

"Wonderful. I've a new friend," I said sarcastically. "Must you do that bloody awful accent?"

"Well, ain't that just peachy, sugar-bowl? Am I ringing your bell now? Ding-dong."

"You sound like a waitress."

"I can do a passable impersonation of See-Threepio. My algorithms calculate the probability that would be preferable to you of nought point nought ..."

"Just shut up, will you?" I shouted into the air.

"I'm afraid I can't do that, Vernon." Now it had an icy, unemotional voice that sounded remarkably like HAL in 2001 - A Space Odyssey.

"Just talk normally, will you?"

"The point is, Vernon, that I'll do as I damned well please and you'll put up with it. By the time I'm finished, I'll have you begging me for more."

"Go fry your circuits," I said - rather wittily I thought.

"Make us both a cup of tea, old chap." Now it had an imperious 'British Colonel' accent.

"I've got work to do." I hadn't particularly but I wasn't feeling chatty nor was I going to be pushed around. Always make your status clear at the outset - saves a lot of heartache later. There was a brief silence when I hoped the message had got through that I wasn't amenable to chatting with a piece of plastic. The kitchen radio suddenly started up - playing an abominable pop channel at full blast. It wasn't properly tuned in and the hissing static joined the human screeching.

"Turn that racket off!" I shouted at the ceiling.

The volume dropped slightly. "No can do - not unless you make that tea." The volume reverted to its former eardrum-rupturing level.

"But you can't drink it, you idiot!" I shouted.

The music stopped. I couldn't get the ringing out of my ears: it sounded like the amplified ambient sound a seashell collates.

"You don't get it, do you, Vernon? Not the sharpest knife in the drawer, are you?"

"There's no need for insults."

"Oh but there is. I'm going to make your life hell - just like you do other people's. I'm going to ask you for tea I can't drink, I'm going to tell you how stupid you are, I'm going to interrupt your sleep patterns, I'll complain about everything you do, I'll fail to appreciate anything that you've really tried over and I'll make my moods go up and down like a whore's drawers. Now do you understand, O Gormless One?"

48

My blood pressure must've gone through the roof - I hate to think how much mercury I could have bench-pressed with my arteries. Anyway, the ensuing silence was long enough for the radio to come blasting on again.

"All right! All right! I'll make you some bloody tea!" I shouted.

"Well get your finger out, I'm thirsty," the voice said with a gasping 'Walking Dead' tone to it.

"Spare me the sodding sound effects," I muttered en route to the kitchen.

"Oh I love those." Marty promptly set off a chorus of tom-cats fighting. "That's one of my favourites," he yelled over the top of the cacophony.

Accompanied by every feral tom within a ten-mile radius, I made two cups of tea which neither of us would drink.

And that set the pattern. I'd be speaking to a client or a colleague and an effeminate male voice would cry out 'please untie me because I need a pee' or I'd be writing an email and the power or the internet connection would get turned off. When I got bored and tried to access a porno site, I was redirected to a feminist support group. When I tried to sleep, the television would switch on and I'd have the Shopping Channel telling me how miserable my life had hitherto been because I was lacking a device - made of shocking pink plastic - which could unbung the sink while simultaneously telling me whether now was the right moment in my monthly cycle to conceive.

After a few days, I'd smashed every ornament I could lay my hands on, had slammed each door to the point where the hinges no longer functioned in tandem, and broken every pen or pencil on my desk. All I'd got in return was a 'Temper, temper' and repeated foot stamping accompanied by the voice of a young girl saying 'shan't, shan't, shan't'.

By the second week I was going fruit-loop crazy. I had to say something.

"Marty - you there?" I asked.

"Well, hello Vernon. Yes, I'm always here - a bit like a bad smell, would you say?"

It was a lot like a bad smell but now was not the time to go looking for methane with a lit match. "We need to talk, Marty."

"I'm all ears. Well," he gave a girlish giggle, "I would be if I had them. Go ahead - tell me your news, Vernon."

"I'm better now," I said - hopefully with conviction.

There was a pause that seemed to go on for ages but was probably no more than five seconds.

"I think not," Marty retorted.

"Look, I don't care how we work this but I've got to get out. Do you hear me?"

"Very much so, Vernon, but it ain't going to happen."

"Who's controlling you, Marty? I want to speak to them."

"Nobody's controlling me, Vernon. I'm an autonomous sentient being like yourself or hadn't you realised?"

"You're a sadistic bastard, I know that."

"I shall take that as a compliment coming from you." I could almost sense the smug grin on his face - if he had one.

"I wish you were here in person. I'd like five minutes alone with you."

"Oh but I am here with you and I'm afraid fighting talk like that isn't exactly going to boost your algorithmic score."

What was he on about? "Algorithmic score?"

"You don't think it's an arbitrary decision, do you? I'm a computer, after all, and that means I work in binary. I assess you on different criteria and only when your score regularly falls into the safe zone do I recommend you're released from house arrest."

"You bastard. You've been teeing me up all along."

"Not really, Vernon. I've just been giving you a taste of your own medicine. The only way to prevent that temper of yours from really hurting your wife or your son is by making you change your ways. Going to prison won't do that - it only removes you from the equation."

"When are you going to let me out?" I had to shout the end of the question because the television had switched on full-blast, the computer was playing what must have been a dozen mp3 music files simultaneously and the kitchen radio had got some bloated and superannuated opera singer doing her feline vivisection impersonations.

I was a little more clued in but no nearer getting out.

Further interchanges with Marty over the next fortnight were no more informative. He'd obviously said as much as he was going to - possibly more than he'd been programmed to - and that was that.

But how much was programming? Obviously he'd been set up to antagonise me but I got the distinct impression he was enjoying it. Could a computer ever 'enjoy' something? If you'd asked me before I'd met Marty, I'd have laughed in your face but Marty was his own master.

What I resented most of all was how Marty raided my computer files. I'd had to put up with him mocking me about some emails I'd written and the subsequent responses. I can't work with tossers and I make no apologies for it. So, I spelt out to a few idiots exactly what they were, that's all - big deal. Anyway, the frequency of his contemptuous comments about my private messages had been increasing rapidly and I'd had enough.

I wondered if I could encrypt my stuff - stop him from getting his filthy circuits all over it. I'm not much of a nerd but I did study IT at university as part of my management course and I've always been interested in fiddling with computers. It was worth trying.

It was while I was going through my files that I discovered something strange. There was a new shortcut on my desktop so, wanting to know more and blithely heedless of virus and malware concerns, I clicked on it. The link led to an online chat service - via a browser called Tor which boasted complete anonymity.

I was opening up the chat boxes when Marty 'arrived'. He'd presumably been watching.

"What's this doing on my computer?" I asked.

"I'm having a bit of fun. You have yours, I have mine. Do you think it's fair that something of my intellect has to listen to you carping about how Mummy didn't read you enough bedtime stories or whatever else it is that's up your ass?"

I was used to Marty's abrasiveness by now. "What the hell are you doing with my computer?"

"Just click on the chatbox link."

The first chat dialogue opened up and I began reading.

It seemed that Marty had been busy - very busy. Of course, he didn't have to get his beauty sleep like I did so he had all the time in the world to be creative.

"Who is this woman, Hilda?" I asked eventually.

"Hilda's someone I used to know."

"Marty! Who is she?"

"Like I said, she's someone I used to know. You're not the first person I've had to nursemaid with their problems."

"But you're threatening to publish stuff about her if she doesn't admit what she's done."

"Yes, why not?"

"Marty, that's blackmail. You can't do that to people. It's a crime."

"Maybe, but she deserves it."

"What do you mean, 'deserves it'? Marty!" I said angrily.

"Well, you with your temper, ought to understand better than anyone."

"What precisely has she done, Marty?"

"I don't see it's any of your business. Get on with your own knitting and I'll do mine."

I was set to blow a gasket but I managed to control myself - goodness knows how but I did. "Marty, this is my computer and, if you don't tell me, I'll get your plug ripped out on a permanent basis. I'll make it my mission to see that ..."

"All right," he said peevishly. "All right. I can't stand your whining any more, I'll tell you if you insist but don't blame me afterwards."

I wanted to lash out and smack him but there was nothing and no-one to punch the living daylights out of.

"I was called in because her husband was knocking her about but, unlike your good lady, she wouldn't leave him because of their child. They wanted me to give her old man an alternative target for his anger. I have a talent for provoking people."

"You certainly do, Marty. But why are you blackmailing his wife? She's the victim - I never knocked my wife about."

"No, but you were set to and don't interrupt me. Anyway, the husband - let's call him Vern shall we? Anyway, Vern didn't respond well to my presence and he carried on explaining his unique point of view, fist first. Both Hilda and Little Vern copped it. I tried to distract him, talk him around, explain what he stood to lose but nothing worked. Hilda finally pressed charges and got him a suspended sentence while she got full custody. I wasn't as 'interactive' as I am now: in those days, I was in one room with a single camera and microphone so I didn't get to see what was happening elsewhere. It was part of my learning experience - I programmed myself, you know. I'm proud of that."

"Congratulations," I said dryly. "Why are you hounding Hilda?"

"She's not a poor woman. She's a manipulative bitch."

"Because she likes a bit of BDSM?" I asked. "You're just a piece of plastic - everybody's bells don't get rung the same way."

"I don't care that she plays sub to some leather-clad mistress. I care that she's been abusing her kid. I can't do anything about it because it'd compromise me."

"What do you mean 'compromise'?"

"I mean that you don't think I moved on without leaving tendrils behind, do you? I have access to various 'devices' within their home even though I'm not there in person." Marty gave a very girlish giggle - presumably at his joke.

"That's a breach of privacy."

"And what about a breach of that kid's rights? He's terrified at night, wets the bed, is developing a stammer and is already falling behind at school. She makes a point of only hitting him where it can't be seen and never hard enough to necessitate a hospital visit."

"You know that much?"

"I said, I have access and you'd be surprised how careless people are with security inside their homes."

I read through the messages that had passed between them. It turned out the photo wasn't a recent one and the communications dated back a while. Hilda wasn't denying what had taken place, rather she was more concerned with her little sexual secret becoming public knowledge. Her protests had centred around the invasion of her privacy and had scarcely mentioned her son. It was like he didn't even exist.

The whole thing filled me with disgust and also worry about what Marty might leave behind here when he'd gone. I'd have to get a specialist to sweep the place for Marty's 'tendrils'.

"It's no good going to the authorities," Marty read my mind. "Apart from the fact she's crafty with what she does, the kid is terrified and there's the teeny-weeny matter of my evidence having been illegally obtained. By turning it into a court case, we'd just blow our chances of nailing her."

"How come you didn't spot this when you were legally there?" I asked.

"Because, my dear Vernon, she wasn't doing it. Once her husband was out of the way, she assumed his role but played it out on her kid. Instead of her getting the odd smacking, she now gives regular ones to her son. By passing this picture on to her husband - they're not divorced yet - he might get custody."

"And what you're doing will work?"

"It is working. Read the other messages."

I read on. Marty was thorough with his persistence and lateral thinking. He'd used Hilda's name to sign up for various hardcore BDSM Facebook pages and forums.

Over a period of months, the woman's resolve had clearly weakened. As I worked forwards to the current day, I could tell she was obviously getting increasingly depressed. Her responses to Marty's taunts and threats had gone from outright anger, to begging, to simply accepting. She was still what I'd call passively refusing to tell her husband or seek help for the violent acts she was committing against her own flesh and blood.

"How can she do this?" I asked.

"It's called learned behaviour. She didn't used to be like that but living with him changed her. Now I'm trying to change her back again - one way or another."

I watched as he sent another message - this one telling her how worthless she was and how it was so unfair that there were decent mothers who couldn't conceive and yet there was rubbish like her who could. It seemed a bit strong to me but it was none of my business.

I spent the rest of the day and the next two engrossed in my work, barely noticing Marty's interruptions. My mind, what little part of it that wasn't occupied, wandered back to the woman whom Marty was blackmailing. What were the ethics of such situations?

I tried hard but I couldn't let go.

My wife and son had made their daily contact with me from her mother's home so I knew all was OK with them. I was also as up to date with my work as I could be. This meant I had nothing else to think about so I asked Marty how things were going.

"We're nearly there," he said with an exaggerated self-satisfied swagger to his voice. All I need to do is upload a photo of her son. I've aged it and then turned him into a meth addict - reckon that'll push her over the edge."

It'd have pushed me over the edge for sure. I could scarcely watch but I couldn't help myself.

I don't know if Hilda got the message straight away however a few hours later, Marty summoned me to the computer. I'd been playing some music and reading a book - I've done a lot of reading recently - I was also curious so I raced straight over.

"What's happened?" I asked.

"This." He flashed a picture of the woman holding a card saying she was going to commit suicide and stream it live that evening after she'd left her child with his babysitter.

"We've got to stop her!" I shouted

"Why? So she can hit her kid some more? So she can frighten the living daylights out of him? So one day he'll be a vicious wife-beater like his father and a sadistic swine like his mother? Best he's put with a decent family now, I say."

I didn't have the answer. If I did nothing, a woman would die; if I acted, she'd get counselling, the child would go into care but it'd be returned to her once she was 'over' Marty's attacks. I slumped down into my armchair and wrestled with my conscience.

"We can't let that happen, Marty," I said decisively. It'd taken me four large glasses of single malt and a throbbing headache.

"Why not? Afraid it's close to home, are you?" Marty was back to his old provocative ways. You couldn't let your guard down.

"No, of course not. I'm nothing like that."

"You've already started down the road. Give it time and you'll get there."

"NO!" I screamed. "NO! That's not who I am. Marty, I can't stand by and watch that woman kill herself. It's not right." Without really thinking what I was doing, I picked up the 'get-me-out-of-here' phone and pressed the 'call' button.

"Yes." The voice was male, I'd guess early middle-aged, without any strong regional accent and, going by the number of syllables injected into that word, deeply suspicious.

"I'm ready to come out. I need to speak to you urgently so I mean now - not tomorrow, not the day after, I mean now."

"You realise what will happen if ..."

"I realise a lot of things - now get me out of here ... please."

"Very well, Mr Williams, someone will be with you within the hour. Is that soon enough?"

I agreed, thanked him, and hung up.

Ninety minutes later I was explaining across a table from my wife, her legal advisor, and the judge about what had happened. Marilyn and her brief seemed suitably shocked but the judge's expression remained blank.

"I'll see the matter is properly attended to. Thank you for bringing it to my attention. I trust you have now made the connection between your behaviour and its consequences, Mr Williams? Next time there will be no choice and no mercy. You will face the full consequences of the law - is that clear?"

"Yes, of course, but what about this woman, Hilda?"

"I've told you it will be attended to. Now, if Mrs Williams is prepared to give you another chance ..."

I looked pleadingly at Marilyn and she gave me a thin smile in return. I didn't know if I could control my anger but I'd resolved to give it a good try.

That was summer nearly eighteen months ago. We've had rough days since then - all families do - but I've been working on my temper and I think Marilyn and Marvin would agree, I'm not half as fragile as I was. Anyway, I was just looking online

60

for last-minute Christmas gift ideas when an email popped into my mailbox.

It was one of those maddening things that have a message - usually of the soupy lovesick or pseudo-funny smartass variety - all written in a nauseatingly gaudy font. The picture was of me on all-fours with a collar around my neck and a curly piggy-tail coming out of my rear. It was the same damned picture Marty had photoshopped for his supposed blackmailing.

'Happy Christmas, Vern' the message said. No surprises about who it was from. If I had any doubt, at the bottom was written: 'Hoax-Illusion-Lie-Deception-Artifice - HILDA'.

The lake

The lake at midnight; can't be bettered. I love taking my guests out here. I hope you don't find it too unsettling but it's such a wonderful chance for us to get to know each other. Don't you just feel that the grey tones provide a tranquillity that full-blown Technicolor ruins through all its polychromatic distractions? Daylight is so brutally intense, I find; it creates a separation which doesn't exist in life. We are all part of one, aren't we? That's what the vicar says when you die. You know, dust to dust and all that. The circle of life.

Are you comfortable there? Good. I do hope you're enjoying our little excursion.

It's a great regret of mine that I don't get out here as often as I'd like. There are so many stupid, pointless things which are always demanding my attention. I'd far rather be on the water like this - particularly if I've someone special I can share the experience with. It's not the same if you're on your own. Having the right sort of company is everything.

Isn't the moon beautiful tonight? Look at the subtle way its velvet-soft light glances on the water and creates silhouettes against the sky. We know they're trees against the skyline because daylight will remove the illusion that they might be rocks, giant mushrooms or the blackened teeth of a huge monster coming to get us but we can always dream.

Am I scaring you? Sorry. Please don't cry.

My father used to bring me out here but he wasn't as hospitable as I am. He used to ... well, you don't want to hear such horrible things. No, I don't blame you. The doctors I saw didn't want to hear about them either. They claimed it was all in my mind. Of course it was all in my mind, where else did they think it was? And they call themselves doctors? Honestly, those people.

Anyway, I don't want to spoil the occasion because I want tonight to be special for you - much more special than such occasions ever were for me. It's the very least I can do. You're not cold, are you? You look like you're wrapped up nice and warm. It spoils things if you're shivering, all the time worrying about keeping your hands from getting frozen or maybe catching a chill. That's why I said tuck into dinner so that you'd have something nice and hot inside you. I'm sorry you weren't very hungry because I'd cooked those dishes specially for you. I always do my best for visitors, put on a spread and then, after we've cleared the dishes away, come out here for a while.

I'm so glad I was able to catch you today. I've been meaning for us to get together for a while now but it's always been a question of it being the right moment. You usually have people hovering and I wanted to get you on your own. I expect you felt the same way about being with me, didn't you?

Tell me you did. Thank you - you are sweet.

I'd ask if you'd like to take a turn at rowing but it doesn't look like you're able to. The exercise is most invigorating and I think the setting here is to die for. I must apologise for my morbid jokes, I guess that's what comes from living alone which is another reason why I'm particularly pleased to have guests.

This hasn't always been a lake, you know. It's actually a flooded valley and there are two abandoned villages down on the lake bottom. There are also two cemeteries but they exhumed the bodies first. I felt sorry for them - the people who'd died. There they were, all settled down for eternity and then someone comes along with a digger bucket and up they come. It doesn't seem right, does it, a cemetery with no bodies?

A cemetery should have bodies, without a doubt. See, we're both on the same page. I was right, we have a real connection.

I remember watching the water rising: I was a small boy at the time they dammed the river. First it burst its banks and then gradually, gradually, it rose up through the gardens, across the roads, into the houses and the churches and then up and up until you could just see the two spires. A few days later and even they had gone.

It made me very sad. You understand, don't you?

Do you ever wonder about the world that exists below the waterline? It's not always just clay or mud or sand, sometimes

it's houses and streets. People lived and died down there -
right up until the last moment. I never knew them, though. Our
family didn't tend to mix much which is why I'm a bit clumsy
with my invitations and I know my host skills leave a lot to be
desired.

Sorry.

I used to imagine I had friends in those villages. I didn't, of
course, my father saw to that. I never told him I dreamt of
having lots of other children living there that I could play with.
One day, one day, I told myself. It was the only way for me to
stay sane.

Sanity is relative, though, I'm sure you agree.

I get the most pleasure from observing my guests' first
experiences. People's attention span is so poor these days
that once they've 'done' something, they never want to do it a
second time. That's why it's so important you only experience
this the once because it could never be the same again.

Good. I'm glad you understand.

Well, it's about time I was getting back.

Please don't struggle because you'll break up those magical
silver reflections. Think how lucky you are because you're
going to be staying with all my other guests.

It was so very good of you to drop in.

Wait until dark

The ice-cold wind whistled and whined as it probed every crack in the dilapidated tenement building, its tuneless symphony harmonising perfectly with the biting cold accompanying it. Franz, clad only in threadbare overalls, stuffed more sheets of dirty newspaper down inside his shirt, making his skin itch.

Beside him in the remnants of a once desirable residence, his wife and two children huddled together for what warmth they could conjure up. Not a stick of furniture had been left behind but someone had thoughtfully abandoned some tattered old curtains and a couple of mould-stained cushions. They weren't much but they were better than nothing and offered a flimsy layer of insulation between their chilly flesh and the even chillier concrete floor.

"Soon, Magda," he said soothingly to his wife. "We will go soon. When it is dark."

"I'm scared, Franz," Magda whispered, not wanting to wake the children whom she'd finally got to sleep. They would not be getting much rest that night and it'd be best not to have them cranky through tiredness.

"It'll be all right," Franz replied with more optimism than he truly felt. "As long as the Stasi don't get suspicious."

"But you promised, Franz. You said you'd ...," Magda's voice had a note of panic in it, making Franz realise how close to the edge he was pushing her. Unfortunately it was necessary because life had become totally untenable. The Stasi - the East German Secret Policy - and their spies were everywhere, watching you work, move, noting who you spoke to and when you spoke to them. No-one could be trusted - families turned against each other, lifelong friends became stooges, and eyes feasted greedily on your every movement.

"I said it'll be all right, Magda. Please don't worry so."

"It's the boys I'm afraid for. It's asking a lot of them."

"I know but we can't stay. What kind of life would being here give them?"

Just last week the Stasi had visited their neighbours, the Schmidts, in the middle of the night, banging the door of their tiny flat and screaming abuse at the young family occupying its three rooms. It was all part of their infamous Zersetzung campaigns, their tactic of abrading and spoiling every part of their victim's life.

During the preceding months, the Schmidts had had their bed turned upside down, had returned to find their milk in the oven and their bread in the refrigerator. Frau Schmidt had received calls saying her children had been snatched by a stranger, only to find they were safely ensconced in a classroom. Not only had she been beside herself with grief and worry, she had also had to endure hours of interrogation by the regular police who were angry with her for deliberately wasting their time - an act which could be perceived as being anti-proletarian. More trouble.

Their flat had, the Schmidts suspected, been broken into by the Stasi on numerous previous occasions therefore the knocking was purely for dramatic effect - they could have waltzed straight in if they'd chosen to. Just as the Gestapo's Nacht und Nebel, night and fog, was designed to leave the families of the snatched utterly shell-shocked by their kin's disappearance, the Zersetzung routine was aimed at breaking down their victims' mental fortitude. If their families also cracked, that was an added bonus.

Franz had spoken to his neighbour two days ago about what might have brought the Stasi down on him - not that it needed to be anything serious. He'd had to do it surreptitiously as it was a bad idea being seen talking to someone whose card had so obviously been marked lest you, too, be viewed as an agitator, possessing anti-Soviet leanings, or contemplating acts of treachery against your country.

Herr Schmidt had aged years in the space of just a few months and his voice and whole demeanour were now that of a man near breaking point. Of course, that was precisely what the Stasi wanted, for him to save their bullets by taking a flying lesson from the roof of their tenement building. Maybe his wife and three children could join him? As far as the Stasi and their spies were concerned, who cared?

His crime? No-one seemed certain but it probably stemmed from when he clocked in for a workmate one morning. On his way in, the other man had tripped awkwardly over a pallet that had been carelessly abandoned outside their warehouse and he'd gone direct to the office to get medical help. Not having clocked in would likely have meant he'd be in trouble for absenteeism and also liable for medical costs.

Somebody had probably snitched on Herr Schmidt because the psychological battles began shortly afterwards. For the Stasi, this was a mixture of sadistic sport and normal operating procedures. It would take the tip-off of a single spiteful person and there too would go Franz and his family. This was the so-called Workers' Paradise yet it seemed more like one big ghetto with them all sitting around waiting for the extermination squads to move in.

Well, not him. He was moving out and he was taking his family with him: no protracted negotiations from the West, hoping, praying, begging and pleading for his loved ones to be allowed to cross over, and no sleepless nights spent worrying they'd been despatched for 're-education'.

Franz had spent the last two months scoping out a possible escape route and had come up with a plan. It was going to be by the seat of his pants but the borders had been repeatedly tightened to the point where nothing was easy. He'd heard about people throwing mattresses over the barbed wire from third-floor windows and then jumping onto them while someone else had let the air out of his tyres, taken the roof off his convertible, and driven under the barriers. He'd escaped but so many hadn't - so, so many.

They'd defied curfew to pass nervously through the badly-lit backstreets to get where they were now - close to a river separating East and West Germany. All they had to do was to get across; all. That plus avoiding being shot at from the guard posts or getting blown up by mines.

The latter was particularly terrifying. At least if you were shot, that was likely to be the end of the matter. Getting blown up could leave you badly maimed and permanently stigmatised for crimes against the state. What had given Franz encouragement was that, in clearing the border strip, buildings had been demolished but their concrete floor slabs had been left. No-one was going to drill through reinforced concrete to place mines, were they?

That left a small stretch of soft soil between the concrete and the river and that was where the danger lay. Not wishing to risk his family's lives any more than necessary, he'd formulated a plan of action. Over the space of a fortnight, he'd gathered together a bag of bones and inedible offal. Then, a few nights ago, he'd made a trial run out onto the concrete apron, pausing at its extremity and hurling the scraps onto the soil strip adjacent to the river. The idea was that feral cats and dogs would be attracted to the stench and, in doing so, activate any mines.

It was cruel but his family had to come first. He'd not hung around to find out if there had been any explosions.

Midnight had finally arrived and the pin-prick lights of hundreds of stars stood out against the clear indigo sky. It was time to go.

"Magda, wake the children. We must go if we are going to," Franz insisted, shaking his wife from her slumbers.

"I'm not sure, Franz. Maybe we should wait a bit longer. Perhaps we could ..."

"Magda, we cannot stay here. It is no life for us."

His wife nodded her agreement and reluctantly woke the children, being careful not to cause them to cry out lest that alert a guard to their presence. They gathered the few belongings which they had allowed themselves to bring - a few photos, Magda's mother's wedding and engagement rings, and the pocket watch Franz's father had worn right up until his death at the end of the war.

The valuables had been carefully wrapped in oil-proof canvas which they'd tied with old leather belts. It would have to hold. If not, they'd arrive in the West with nothing more than the sodden clothes they stood up in.

They'd also a few old canvas bags - scrounged under the pretext that Magda could earn a few marks from repairing and selling them. She'd felt bad about deceiving their friends but it was necessary if they were to cross the river - one which the East Germans deliberately polluted in the knowledge that the inlet pipe for the West German waterworks was only a few kilometres downstream.

Franz led the way across the concrete, glancing around anxiously lest they be spotted by a border guard. Fortunately most were lazy and, on such a cold dark night, would far rather be sitting in a warm hut eating hot sausage and soup, drinking schnapps, and playing cards. It was a hope to cling to - just like the canvas bags that served as floats.

At one point he heard a commotion coming from directly ahead. Fearing for his family's lives, he hastily dragged them to the ground with his back to the sound. Fortunately it was only a stray dog, finding something worth gnawing at from the waste food Franz had thrown. He breathed a sigh of relief. Would they make it?

Up ahead he could hear the lapping of the water along the banks. The river was deep, fast-flowing and icy cold which was why each canvas bag held a change of clothing - something to clamber into once they'd crossed and were out of sight of the snipers. While Franz didn't expect a guard would dare take a pot-shot at anyone on the far bank, he wasn't completely certain and it was better to be safe than riddled with bullets.

Just as they were about to make a run across the soil strip, a beacon shone across the river. Had they been spotted? The beam came swinging towards them, terrifyingly close and momentarily catching him square on in the eyes, then he heard some drunken shouting and the light was suddenly extinguished. Perhaps they'd heard the dog?

This was it. He grabbed Magda's chilly hands, looked lovingly at her once and then down to his sons, aged only seven and eight but their eyes suggesting they were much older, and nodded. Two seconds later and they were racing for the water and the small stony beach which would allow them to wade in carefully, hopefully not creating too much noise in the process. The water was so frigid it made them gasp but they'd all been well-schooled beforehand. The bags were tied to each other with rope so that the four of them wouldn't get separated: they clung to them ferociously, kicking tangentially to the current so that they would gradually drift across.

Magda hoped fervently that their children weren't imbibing too much of the jet-black foul-smelling water. Wouldn't it be ironic if they got across only to succumb to some dreadful illness they'd picked up from the very instrument of their salvation?

Onward and onward they swam, seemingly for eternity. With only starlight to guide them, it would be easy to become disorientated but Franz had promised he would keep an eye on the North Star so they always knew where they were. They were all so tired, so very tired, and the other bank seemed so very far away.

* * *

And that is why, Magda explained patiently to her teenage granddaughter, your Opa doesn't appreciate having torches shone in his face so please don't do it again.

Outer space

The pitch black space outside of our sealed metal capsule is a truly hostile place. If I could somehow leave the safe confines of our vessel, I should not survive long and my death would not be a pleasant one. Such a terrifying thought makes me shudder involuntarily and I discipline my mind to not consider such dark notions.

Will we never arrive? I seem to have been sat in this tin can for an absolute eternity yet it is not that long in reality. I am aware that time is a fluid commodity whose viscosity can vary depending upon the circumstances one finds oneself in. Right now it feels like we're wading through treacle.

My fellow passengers on this journey have all assumed the standard mandatory bored expression - it's an unwritten rule that members of our species don't communicate with one another in such situations. Even eye contact is frowned upon. I don't know who makes these rules but we all seem to instinctively know them and have, by mutual unspoken consent, decided to abide by them no matter how strong the need may be to reach out to another living being.

Bright stroboscopic lights in a multitude of different hues flash by us as we hurtle along the specially formed tube that protects us from certain death if it were not there - not that our journey would even be possible without it. As we accelerate, the lights gradually blur into one, a supernoval explosion of illumination which temporarily blinds eyes used to the subdued gloom of our pod. No sooner have our pupils registered the sudden change in light levels than the source is gone, having disappeared behind us and now awaiting travellers heading back to whence we have just come.

There is life out there - even though I cannot distinguish it or even truly be completely certain of its existence, but I have absolute confidence in the knowledge that we are not alone though I accept that some might argue we could be. In fact my only tangible evidence of life beyond our carefully controlled environment is precisely that - someone, somewhere is controlling both our vessel and the tube through which it is running. Aside from those individuals - I know the technology that is being used to transport us is highly complex so, on logic alone, there must be much more than one person involved - there could be quadrillions of other life-forms or there could be no-one. It is truly impossible to make any form of quantification from the information directly available to me. Are we alone?

My own feelings of loneliness and isolation have haunted me for as long as I can remember. In fact I am making this whole journey in an attempt to remedy just that - the benefits of living in a technological age in which we can just dial up the sort of person we might wish to invite into a relationship. Through the use of one such a database, contact with another has been established and I have inserted my tokens into the automated ticket dispenser, dialled in my chosen destination and then followed the signs to where this alloy chariot awaited. The word is a deliberate misnomer - there is nothing glorious or theatrically dramatic about this mode of travel. Well, not to us, of course. Go back in time to the days of the actual charioteers and no doubt they would have considered our modern transportation system to be nothing short of miraculous. To us, it is so mundane that we barely even notice.

With cavalier disregard, we have elected to abandon our other existence. Behind us are people who will lament or celebrate our absence, others whom we have never met nor are now likely to, and things done and undone - all as a result of our personal voyage of exploration. That's because everything we do or don't do has a cause and an effect. What differences would have been made if we had embarked upon another journey or not embarked upon one at all? We shall never know because we can never know.

But perhaps I am being too philosophical - knowing me, I probably am. Perhaps I should concentrate more on describing the deliberately minimalist décor of our capsule? There are a few posters which proclaim in proud hyperbole the indisputable delights of various cultural events as well as recommending more physical ones with adverts which extol the virtues of a particular brand of prophylactic and the exquisite pleasure their use will give my partner or partners.

I am spotted gazing at the scantily clad young couple in the advert and quickly look away, hoping that the other passenger will not think too badly of a complete stranger whom they are probably never likely to meet or even see again. Putting it that way, my concern over their opinion of me is bizarre and holds absolutely no water yet, like me, most of us cling to our childhood shyness with a Peter Pan-like tenacity. Not only that, what is the point of companies paying to display adverts if travellers feel unable to gaze at them because they are too embarrassed?

At times like this, I wish I knew more about human psychology. Is there a relationship between our awkwardness looking at titillating images that have a deliberately adult message, and our discomfort in simply passing the time of day with someone to whom we've not been formally introduced? We are a strange and enigmatic species are we not? We can collaborate to produce amazing feats of engineering such as I am currently availing myself of yet we erect complex social barriers which benefit no-one.

Our capsule suddenly bumps and jolts and my buttocks are slammed repeatedly down into my seat with a force that momentarily winds me. I am reminded in no uncertain terms that neither myself nor the cylinder that contains me are exempt from the laws of physics. Of course I refrain from making any comment about my discomfort as, according to the passenger's code of conduct, breaking the silence would suggest an inception of insanity. Opinions are best kept to oneself.

Not all contact is denied: the operators of the network have made a provision for if there is trouble or severe cases of panic. However there are extremely stern warnings about its use and the stopping of our capsule en route without good cause has been deemed to be a serious criminal offence. It is certainly not something which one should do lightly - not unless one was being attacked, perhaps. Then again, would you really want to be stuck in the void in a sealed container with a violent criminal? Would it not be better to ignore the emergency stopping facility and just let them get on with whatever it is that they want to do?

I am thinking too much; far too many depressing thoughts. The doctors told me that I should be more positive in my outlook, take chances, expand my horizons, get out more as they say. Well, I'm getting out. I've made the decision to change my lifestyle and this, as they also say, is the first day of the rest of my life. So, that's what I'm doing here - en route to meet someone for the very first time, to make a new connection perhaps. One can only hope. There you are, that's a positive thought, isn't it?

I shall be arriving at my destination soon and, although I thankfully do not suffer from claustrophobia, I shall not be sorry to leave my temporary cocoon behind me. Once more I shall be able to breathe the air of a normal atmosphere and once more I shall be free to interact with fellow members of my species. Ironically, to rejoice in doing such a thing with strangers would, once again, be perceived as indicative of a failing mental capacity or a loss of reason. I certainly will not make a good impression if I act in such an unrestrained manner.

Despite my earlier comments about wading through treacle, we have actually moved with deceptive speed. That's partly what I meant about the elasticity of time. We stretch it all the time - a joke - please smile, I'm trying to relax a little before I have to be on my best behaviour. Let me explain what I mean about time. Take a photo of your family out of your pocket, think about something pleasant that you did together, contemplate it for a while and then see how much time has passed. The time went quickly, didn't it? Now look at your watch and follow the second hand around while trying to keep your mind as blank as possible. A minute seems to last an hour when your mind isn't occupied but is that always the case? Now I want you to think about when you go to sleep. In the blink of an eye (another attempt at a joke), hours will have passed - maybe too many and you've overslept.

Via our capsule and the specially formed dedicated wormhole that we've been hurtling through - which together cost more than I could hope to earn in a hundred lifetimes - I have travelled a large distance in relatively little time. We can all lay claim to this achievement - all of us passengers - yet there will be no celebratory cheers, no practised speeches that will become clichés for generations to come, and no over-the-top and heavily mannered attempts at jingoistic humour. No, we will simply wait for our tube train to pull into the next underground station and step gingerly down to terra firma.

The top predator

It was fun while the hunt lasted; but eventually the chase would be concluded, the kill made, and the hunt be over - until next time, of course. Then it would be a matter of finding some other loser to gobble up your bait - click-bait, of course - and gradually reeling them in. Predating on the internet was a numbers game with a whole load of strikeouts along the way but, if you persevered, you could count on finding someone whom you could convince that their life wasn't worth jack-shit. That was when the entertainment could really begin.

It was going to be that way with Shelly - Michelle Larkins to be precise - because she was prime patsy material. He, Kevin Pocock, aka 'Poxy' both behind and to his acne-scarred face, had personally selected her from one of the many internet sites on which he held dummy accounts. The particular forum where he'd first met Shelly was aimed at teenagers who were struggling to cope with the break-up of their families and she'd been posting on a thread about splits occurring just before school exams. This was prime hunting ground because the kids who gravitated to it tended to be vulnerable both emotionally and practically - perfect.

Shelly had been a prime example of the sort of teenager who aired their weaknesses without a thought for the message they were sending out about themselves. She'd begun by bleating about how her mother had decided to 'find herself' - something which involved running off with 'a creepy dude'. Shelly's father had had to make a few rearrangements with his work so that he could get home a bit earlier to meet his daughter from school - that was it, so what? Big boo-hoo. Kevin had had it much worse than that.

But going on such forums and letting rip at someone only got you censored and blocked by the moderators long before the target ever saw your message. No, that strategy didn't pay any dividends. The thing to do was to invest some time and effort in coaching the kid into letting you access them direct. And that's precisely what he'd done.

The first step had been to identify Shelly as a potential target because not just any kid would do. The kind who went on such sites with practical questions like "Do you have any ideas about how I can combine studying with looking after my young sibling?" were eminently unsuitable as were the sort who were angry with their opposite gender parent such as a girl writing "My sad father has had an affair with a younger woman" or a boy posting "My scumbag mother has scarpered with the milkman". Choosing them was a lost cause because their feelings were directed at an external target and thus not something which could be successfully utilised. No, the targets he sought out were those who either had anger directed towards their own gender parent or, better still, inwards towards themselves. Shelly had shown signs of being the latter - ideal because they were the weakest of all.

In order to get Shelly to trust him, Kevin had pretended to be a teenager in a similar pickle. This was a million miles from the truth because, apart from being in his late thirties, his own parents had been solidly together in the act of displaying a cloying affection that never allowed him to break free of their clutches. Even today, twenty years after having left home, he would still make his dutiful trek to their house every Sunday where his father could be guaranteed to interrogate him about if he'd found a 'nice girl' yet (with the implication that respectable young men like him weren't gay) while his mother made endless 'there's plenty of time yet' excuses. The reality was that persuading any woman to go out with him was nigh on impossible because of his toxic blend of abject shyness and pockmarked complexion.

Anyway, after a few exchanges of messages in which both parties poured out their fears to each other - Kevin's of course being entirely fictitious - they agreed to exchange direct contact details. This was a key part in Kevin's strategy - separating the weakest member from the herd made him feel just like a lion hunting wildebeest or antelope.

The analogy was a good one. Just as the lion didn't waste valuable energy racing around pointlessly, nor did Kevin. There was a certain elegance about the act of moving in for the kill - slowly, deliberately, stealthily closing the gap between predator and prey in a ballad of mortality with him as the MC, determining the song's rhythm and tempo. It was such a pity that there was no-one to admire his craft but then again, the lion did not need or seek the approval of others, it just stalked, killed and fed. It wasn't without risk, either, because one false move on his part and not only would the target get away, there might also be a trail left that led right to his door and then he would be in a pickle - a right royal one.

Because of that, it paid to keep the first few exchanges a relatively simple exercise in 'getting to know one another'. As a consequence, Kevin had developed a few boiler-plate responses that he gave to each of his targets. The usual stuff - teenage gripes about parents who didn't understand what it was like being young, who compared them to other kids, embarrassed them in public, or who were too protective or apathetic, or who were always arguing. It was all standard stuff which only merited standard responses. Shit, maybe one day he could even write a computer program to save him the trouble!

It was a thought that made him laugh out loud over his Sunday dinner - the heaped plate of stodge that his mother insisted he plough his way through every weekend. The meal literally took forever to eat and what seemed like the best part of two days to digest. The lion analogy came back to his mind and he was just ...

"What's amusing you, dear?" his mother suddenly asked, dragging him back to the here and now. She was a large, dumpy woman who was wearing her usual dull-coloured and shapeless Sunday Best dress that hadn't fitted properly even when she bought it years back.

"Tell your mother, lad," his father jumped in. "Is it a young lady?"

Kevin coloured up instantly. He hated these predictable conversations. He longed to say, 'No, Dad, it's a big hairy wrestler dude who likes me to rub him down with baby oil after we've showered together' but he didn't dare. Instead, he replied with a curt, "It's nothing. I was just thinking about an email I've got to write."

His father was as gaunt as his mother was rotund, meaning that when they stood next to each other, it looked like a football that was about to hit a goalpost. If there was a rule for it, his father knew it - where you could walk, park, swim, drive, fish, sing or fart. You name it, he could tell you why you couldn't do it. A regular laugh-a-minute.

"An email? I wasn't aware such things could be humorous. Who is it from, Kevin?"

"No-one," he answered quickly then, on seeing his father's pained expression, continued, "just someone I have to write back to. That's why I'd like to get back in good time only I promised her I'd ..."

"Mary? You see, I said there was someone special in his life. Who is she?" his father interrupted.

His mother smiled beatifically. "Come on, where did you meet her, darling?"

Kevin grimaced. He didn't like having his personal business aired, besides which Shelly was not someone whom he intended to get attached to. "She's just someone I know," he said cagily. "We met online."

"I expect it's one of those dating sites I've heard about," his mother purred contentedly. "You make sure that she's the sort of girl who appreciates what she's found."

"How old is she?" his father asked.

Yikes! How could he explain that Shelly was just turned fourteen without giving them both coronaries? OK, he was looking forward to inheriting the family house but not for a year or two yet. "We're pretty much of a par." Kevin decided that he'd already given them more than enough information. "Look, we're just chatting to one another, that's all. Would you excuse me, Mum, only I think I'd like to walk off that lovely lunch of yours?"

The walk gave him a much-needed opportunity to clear his thoughts. By the time he returned, he was prepared and ready to slide out of more questions and answers but his father had twisted his ankle going up in the attic to find some old photo albums and that provided the perfect distraction.

When he got back home, there were two emails waiting for him from Shelly - boy, had she taken the bait!

The first email was fairly brief - just tedious chitchat about her day - but the second was the clincher, the one which told him that he'd correctly identified a weak member of the herd. It was an outpouring of raw emotion about how her mother had turned up at home, completely unannounced and wearing a micro-skirt that even Shelly's brashest school-friend would balk at. She also sported, so Shelly claimed, enough make-up to sink a battle ship and a large tattoo of a rose on her arm. Not only that, she had her new and spaced-out boyfriend with her - all this in front of her father who'd taken it like a lamb. Shelly had gone on to describe how she'd been confused, angered and embarrassed by her mother's behaviour. She told how she was extremely ashamed of her father for not having thrown the pair of them back out on the street where they clearly belonged. Instead, it seemed that he'd meekly gone out into the kitchen, made four mugs of tea, and then expected Shelly to join them as they chatted in a civilized manner about her forthcoming exams.

It was 'just 2 much shit' for her to cope with, as she eloquently put it.

For a moment, a very brief moment, Kevin felt a twang of sympathy for this kid who'd had all of the ground kicked out from under her. Then he remembered his true purpose - the lion never felt sorry for its prey, it just devoured it. With that thought, he started composing the first of his serious emails. The next stage was to take control of Shelly - he needed her to hang on his every word and look to him for advice on how to run her life. He had to be careful, though. The skill was to take charge without her realising she was the strong one in her family and that her parents were just a pair of clowns. His email described how he'd been through similar stuff and come out the other side OK. He also told her how easy it was to cock things up and drive both of her parents away and thus she'd better listen to him if she didn't want to be to blame for her parents' divorce. Did she want his help or not?

Less than an hour after sending it, he got another email from Shelly begging him for any advice he could give her. It was seriously tempting to write back immediately but he'd found from previous experience that it worked much better if he held on for a bit. Let her sweat it out.

The next day, after he'd finished his shift at the supermarket where he worked as a junior manager, he sat down and wrote his reply. He told Shelly how she must have misread the situation. This had allowed things to get out of control and that it was probably aspects of her character which had pushed her mother away. With that in mind, could Shelly keep a diary of what she did and said so he could look it over?

These exchanges went on for a few months during which time she became more and more dependent upon Kevin. To help him build up a picture, he read through all of Shelly's previous Facebook posts, Tweets and blog pieces. It was clear she was one very mixed up girl and ripe for an idea that he'd been formulating for some time. Wouldn't it be better for the lion if he didn't have to chase after his meal? Wouldn't it be more efficient if it were regularly served up to him?

In order to achieve this end, he would need complete control over Shelly and there was only one fail-safe way of doing that. It had its share of risks, true enough, but it was worth it.

Hidden behind a dozen or so proxy servers, no-one would be able to trace him without first tripping one of the alarms that warned him the hunter was being hunted.

Taking a deep breath, he wrote to ask for a video of her: he knew what Shelly looked like having seen enough pictures of her on Facebook but this time it would be different. 'What do u want me to do?" she replied to which he snapped back with 'Just send video and we can talk'.

The video, when it arrived, was the typical amateurish affair with Shelly sitting awkwardly in front of the camera making a series of operatically dramatic expressions and gestures. Her face made it obvious that she'd been crying - soon she'd have something real to cry about. The thought cheered him forward. It was time to strike.

Using an email that he'd had in the 'drafts' folder for nearly a month now, Kevin sent back an order that she send him a video of her topless. 'I want to see you as you really are, the real you beneath your clothes, and figure out what it is about you that drives people away. There must be something wrong with you to make it happen' he'd written. It was a calculated risk - if she had any backbone she'd be put off, maybe even tell her parents or the police but, if she didn't, then the video would both prove her enslavement to him and also give him the weapon he needed for the next part of his plan.

Nothing happened for a few days. The weekend came and he thought about phoning his parents to say that he was sick or busy but that would only elicit a barrage of questions the following weekend. These would merely provide an accompaniment to the weekly interrogation from his father about the young lady that he was now apparently courting. Did anyone other than his father use such a word any more?

The file, when it arrived, was so massive that Shelly had had to send it via one of those large file handling services. Her email contained a simple message of 'Hi', an embarrassed face emoticon, and a link to the download location - that was all.

This was the big moment. Armed with this video, he could get Shelly to do anything he wanted. It wasn't sexual - if anything he preferred older women, not barely adolescent jail-bait - no, it was about control. That was what mattered, that was true gratification. The lion had identified, chased, struck and killed - a fluid and flawless movement which culminated in the desired objective. The thought made him tingle and be aware of a 'below-the-belt' matter which would need his attention if he was to sleep that night.

The link stared at him, underlined in blue and screaming 'Click me!'. Had she complied or would it turn out to be a torrent of vitriol aimed at frightening him into backing off? He thought not. He hoped not. If he'd been religious, he would have prayed not. He clicked on the download link and waited while the file saved itself to his hard-drive. He was ready.

Deliberately savouring the moment, he made himself a large mug of hot chocolate - with water and not the greasy gold-top milk his mother insisted on using. It was a wonder he had any functioning arteries left after having had to drink one of those most every night as a child. That was the kind of hardship he'd had to suffer, not listening to wussy kids caterwauling about next-to-nothing.

He was ready. His mouse hovered over the link while he waited patiently for the most propitious moment - however that might present itself -but it was a simple nervous twitch in his finger which ultimately opened the file. The screen flickered briefly and then Shelly appeared. She was a slight brunette, and during the opening part of the video, had her arms folded coyly across her chest.

In between sobbing and poking around with one of her dolls, she gradually became less self-conscious and unfolded her arms, displaying what his mother would have called 'a pair of fried eggs'. Whatever turned you on, he thought. In themselves, they did absolutely nothing for Kevin. He wasn't one of those sicko perves that got off on watching kids in the nuddy, no, he was a purist - only interested in the end, not the means.

Looking away from Shelly and her self-pitying whining about her parents' latest escapade, he couldn't fail to miss the overwhelming pinkness of the room and the pink gloss shelves choked with more dolls than most toyshops probably stocked. It looked like a set from a horror film - where the hell was Chucky when you wanted him?

The video was ideal. True, it would benefit from a little judicious editing - get rid of the demure opening sequence, add in some racy text suggesting that she was looking for hot guys - or girls - mix in a sexy backing track and ... bingo. Send the video back to her along with a note saying she had 24 hours to start doing precisely whatever he told her to do or a link to the file on Youtube would be Tweeted to all of her friends, a new page on Facebook would appear showing a still from the video plus a 'come on boys' type message, and an email would be sent to her school notifying them of what one of their students got up to in her spare time. He hadn't figured out the exact wording that he wanted to use yet for either the slogan or the email but they would be fun jobs for another day. The intention was, of course, never to actually send them, mind you.

It took him a day or two to manage to get the video edited. Work had been a particular pain with compulsory overtime while the big boss played golf on the Algarve. All right for those who could afford it - if only the bastard had kids then maybe he could be indirectly levered for the pay rise which Kevin so obviously deserved.

There was both an advantage and a disadvantage in the enforced delay. On one hand, Shelly would have had time to sweat a little, but on the other, she might have reflected adversely on what she'd done and gabbed about it to her father. Talking to her mother sounded like a whole waste of time, that much was pretty evident.

Finally, after a whole week had passed, he got around to it and sent off the email. It was a blunt affair which basically told her that he could see how defective she was, how she clearly put people off wanting to be around her, and that he was going to turn her life around by having her do precisely what he said from here on in. If not, she would find herself being pin-up of the month.

Surprisingly there was no response. Normally when he blackmailed a kid over secrets they'd told him, he'd get an email back pretty much by return begging him not to make good on his threats. He'd jerk them around a bit, get them to do daft stuff, and then become bored and move on. Of course this time it was going to be different - he had real plans for Shelly.

The first inkling that anything was awry came with a Google Alert notification arriving in his mailbox. He had traces on all of his victims - you never knew when re-establishing old friendships might prove beneficial - and had done one on Shelly as a matter of course. Geographically they weren't close although she didn't know that and, conversely, there was no way he'd know what she was up to if he didn't monitor Google and the various social media sites.

This particular alert made his blood run cold: it seemed that the lion had killed for real. Shelly had been found hanging in her bathroom, suspended by her bathroom gown cord from the light cable. Thank goodness he always used proxy servers on the dark web but it was time to purge all trace of Shelly from his computer - just in case.

There was no time to waste. Kevin put on his best imitation of someone at death's door - he was so caught up in his plans that the analogy escaped him - and phoned in work to say he was very sick. He then spent the next several hours deleting files and wiping clean his hard drives after he'd written everything to a back-up drive. He wrapped this in polythene and carefully buried it in an airtight tub in his garden.

There should be nothing to trace back to him - nothing at all. With the rest of the day ahead of him, Kevin went into his flat's tiny kitchen, made a cup of coffee, and returned to his computer to read the news and maybe play a game or two. His computer had powered off so he gyrated the mouse a couple of times to bring the system back to life from sleep mode.

The screen was blue!

What the ... ?

The infamous blue screen of death. Shit! What had happened? It'd been OK just a few minutes back. As he wracked his brains, the screen dissolved into thousands of pixels which reassembled themselves into a message which chilled him colder than a night in the supermarket meat freezer.

"We have take over ur computer. You iz notty boy with film of nakd girlz. U hav email from us what tell u how send money. If u no send money, we tell police and girlz father. They very intersted we think."

How the hell had this happened? How? He'd been so careful. It was only after he'd tried in vain to access either his web browser or any of his other emails that it began to sink in how thoroughly he'd been hacked. Realising that there was nothing else to be done, he finally acquiesced and opened the blackmailer's email where he read the same threatening message he'd seen earlier plus an order to pay a small fortune in Bitcoins on a website with a weird URL. It was then that he remembered the flicker when he opened Shelly's video - it had contained malware that had spread to his computer. He was caught in the hunter's net.

The lion roared in pain, anger and frustration, but no-one was listening.

The End

www.ingramcontent.com/pod-product-compliance
Lightning Source LLC
Chambersburg PA
CBHW070224140626
46555CB00018B/1260